THE BOOK OF
THREE

By Dobie Holland

THE BOOK OF
OF
THREE

THE BOOK OF THREE

Copyright © 2014 by Dobie Holland

Cover by: Lewis Lee

ISBN: 978-0-692-24713-6

Book Website
www.dobieholland.com

Give feedback on the book at:
twitter@dobiesterio

Printed in U.S.A

To the members of the
Holland clan no longer with us:
Mama, Daddy, Mona & Lottie.
Love always…

Acknowledgements

I would like to thank God for blessing with me with the parents and family and friends I have met along the way, because without them, none of this would have been possible.

I would like to give a shout out to the Holland family, my brothers Larry, Andrew, John, Leroy, Jimmie, Willie and Curtis; and my sisters, Romona, Dianne, Lottie, Albester and my parents, Estella and Curtis. A big shout to all the nieces and nephews, cousins, aunts and uncles,

I would like to acknowledge Lewis Lee for his tireless work and brilliance in cover design and Brian Peterlinz, for all his help and inspiration for the Christopher Banks character. A big thank you to my Johnson Publishing Company family, namely, Clarence Waldron Trudy Moore, Margena Christian, Jean Williams, Katara Washington, Veronica Clemons, Ronald Childs, Willie Wofford, Lou Ransom, Malcom West and the late great Robert E. Johnson for helping to shape me as a reporter, a writer and an editor over the years.

I would like to thank Timothy Broderick, Jeremy Murti and Melvin Chong for their input and unwavering support. You guys helped in ways I could never have imagined and you are very much appreciated.

Chapter 1
Happy Birthday

I was born in the projects and I can remember when it was a nice place to live. I grew up on the South Side of Chicago, and more importantly, I lived on State Street—that great street.

Like most African-American families living in Chicago in the 1960s, my parents emigrated from the Deep South. They hailed from Clarksdale and Greenville, Mississippi and made the exodus in 1944. Of the tens of thousands of families that vied for the privilege of living in the marvelous new housing Mecca, known as the Robert Taylor Homes— my family was one of the chosen few accepted.

The Taylor Homes were 16 stories of maroon and white concrete. When I was a kid, they reminded me of Rodan—a giant prehistoric-like bird with a condor crown and powerful wings. The bird's body was the structure's centerpiece with no residences, but the wings were full of them. Eight units on each side with steel balconies piled sixteen stories high.

I lived on 5326 South State Street in apartment 103. I was taught my name and address and phone number when I was three and a half years old so I never forgot it. The mean streets of Chicago were pretty tame compared to nowadays, but nothing could compare to the woes and perils I faced from my older brothers and sisters.

One of my early childhood moments occurred when I was four years old. The great blizzard of 1967 dumped piles and piles of white powder on the city that works, bringing it to a grinding halt

1

as people abandoned their cars, trucks and even buses in the streets and scurried inside their warm and toasty nests for hot cocoa with tiny marshmallows.

For us kids, big and small, it was a winter wonderland. Snow clung to every inch of every object around. The monkey bars in the playground had an extra covering and every car for miles wore a blanket of thick white fluffy powder—even street lamps were weighted with it. My mother wrapped me in three sweaters, an overcoat, and a full-body navy snow suit, with matching galoshes. I walked around like some kind of snow mummy—all two feet of me. The snow came up to my head and chest when I ventured out with my brothers and sisters, who were equally wrapped up. My older siblings were hurling snowballs and rolling snow men into place. And I tried to do my favorite thing, making snow angels but unfortunately that was a bad idea. I was literally buried alive and I couldn't see a thing. I screamed and screamed for help, but all I could see was the cold dew from my breath and the feel of cold white powder all around me. Finally my big brother John and my sister Dianne dug me out, dusted me off and took me in the house for some of that hot chocolate with the miniature marshmallows.

I can remember the smell of fresh baked bread and sweet rolls in our neighborhood in the mornings, courtesy of the Dolly Madison bakery nearby. During that fateful blizzard in '67, we had a stroke of good luck. A large delivery van dared to deliver the goods on this day and tipped over on its side. The driver, a bearded white man with a Bella Lugosi accent, climbed out unscathed and helped hand out trays of baked sweet rolls, pastries and bread to the people, who rushed to his aid. We had about four-dozen glazed sweet rolls and donuts to consume. It was glorious man.

In the summer of '67 there were more action-packed incidents in my young life than I care to remember but this one I'm about tell you about is unforgettable. I was rudely awakened from a peaceful mid-day slumber in my room. I slipped on my PJ Flyer sneakers and followed the loud noise which seemed to be coming from the living room. I could hear Dianne's voice screaming at the top of her lungs, "leave me alone Lil John.

My brother John is a mischievous prankster, who will go the distance for a good laugh. "Leave me alone boy," Dianne shouted again, equally as ear piercing.

"C'mon Dianne, what you gonna do, "John shouted back as he shadow boxed around her like Muhammad Ali. Dianne took a swing at him but he stepped back deftly out of the way. I could sense John was nearer to me by the corner of the hallway so I decided to come out and take a look.

Dianne reached for a fluffy floor pillow and hurled that at him. But John caught it and flicked it aside to emphasize just how futile her efforts were.

If my Taurus sister could get any angrier, she just did so she picked up a large medal ashtray that was about eighteen inches long with a heavy metal base; she hoisted the monstrous container overhead, cocked it back and launched it at John.

This is the same John, who hung off the side of the Bob roller-coaster at Riverview Amusement Park for a better thrill, so he easily dodged the projectile. I was not so lucky, because I stepped in the hallway to intervene and right into the path of the mighty metal menace.

I heard a loud thump as the ashtray collided with my forehead. Amazingly, I stayed on my feet but I was seeing red stars—no, more like lightening streaks.

Now I was furious, I shouted, "I'M TELLING ON YOU!

Dianne and John both stopped in their tracks and looked at me in a way that mortified me.

Tears came to her eyes as she sobbed out "I'm sorry Dobie."

My face was hot and the tears were thick in my eyes. I wiped them away and looked at my hand. Wait a second I thought, this ain't like no tears I've ever seen before. This is BLOOD!!!

I screamed and ran through the hallways as if I were suddenly on fire. I ran from one end of the hallway to the other but the blood kept squirting out of my head like water from a water pistol.

Dianne followed me around trying to hug me and comfort me, but I was inconsolable. I ran into her bedroom, jumped on her bed and writhed in agony. Wailing, like a banshee, I managed to scream, "you are gonna get the devil beat out you when mama and daddy get home", and I passed out.

I awoke on a hospital gurney, there were straps across my chest and feet as the ER doctor stitched me up as good as new. It took five stitches to close the wound just underneath my hairline.

My sister and brother got the whippings of their lives for that, so I was told, and John received a week's grounding for starting the whole messy ordeal. It hardly seemed like a fitting punishment, since I carry that scar around till this day.

On April 4, in the Year of Our Lord 1968, I achieved the greatest milestone in my young life—I turned five years old. To commemorate this occasion, I would have a birthday celebration to end all celebrations.

I was a bright, cute, precocious and happy child—the eleventh of twelve children and the eighth and youngest son. Our neighbors and friends in the 'hood would call us the "Dirty Dozen" after the famous war movie.

My eldest sibling is Albester; technically she is the second born child to Curtis and Estella Holland, because Lily Sue was the first. She died of scarlet fever a few months after birth. She was 22 years old on January of that year and is the family elder. We all call her Al and she is very intelligent and goal oriented woman who is fair and has a lovely smile.

She will work for the federal department of health, education and welfare for more than thirty years. She and her new husband Eddie Hall have a seven-month-old daughter named Brenda—my first niece of many to come.

My second eldest sibling is my sister Lottie Mae. She was born March 23, 1947 and she has just turned 21 at the time of my birthday. We are fellow Aries. She and her husband Spencer Lee Dawson have a son, Spencer, Jr. He is nine months old and my first nephew of many. We would give him the nickname of "Bumpsie" because he had a habit of bumping his head on things. Lottie is dark-skinned with striking features. She is very outgoing, very talkative and smart as a whip. She loves barbecue takeout and gossiping. But she is wise and fun-loving.

My brother Curtis Jr. or Curt is next in line. He is my oldest brother and is quick to remind everyone in the family. He is taller than my parents at five-feet, ten inches, with light brown complexion. I think he also has the best smile in the family. His perfectly straight white teeth can light up a room, which is why I think he is always the life of the party. At this point, he is a bachelor who recently moved out of the house into a two-bedroom flat in the South Shore community. He is also working and attending Loop College. Curt was born on July 22, 1948 so you do the math on his age at this time.

My second eldest brother Willie is next on the family tree. He was born November 28, 1949, and he is respectfully called "Rock." A champion swimmer and avid nature lover, the brown skinned Rock is only five feet, five inches, but built like an Adonis. His gap-toothed smile would flash from behind a mustache at a moment's notice. He has a very good sense of humor and his kid-at-heart demeanor makes him very popular with us kids.

My bro Jimmie is Holland number five and he was born February 26, 1951. He is the tallest person in our family at six feet, one inch and he is very athletic. He was tall dark panther of a man and a basketball star at Du Sable High School, but his career is about to end by the fall when he will decide to drop out of school.

Leroy is next in line born on June 26, 1952. He is nicknamed Jolly because he is chubby, but his brown skinned appearance is deceptive. He is quite clever and would land a job with the Post Office just out of high school.

My brother John is next and we simply call him Lil John. My parents call him John L., which is his middle initial, however it has no other meaning. He would surprise those who dubbed him as little as he would grow to nearly six feet tall and become a formidable basketball player for Du Sable High. Grades, however, would kill his athletic hoop dreams. He would become one of the legendary playground ballers of his day. He shares the same birthday as Curt, but he was born five years later in 1953.

Dianne, the famous ashtray hurler, is probably my closest sibling in my adult life. Yes I forgave her for cracking my noggin. She was born on May 13, 1955 and she is about to turn 13 years old next month.

Andrew, who we called Drew, was born January 20, 1958. He and John shared a bed while me and Larry, born November 19, 1959, shared the other bed in our room. How comfy was that, not very but it was the only way I knew.

I was born April 4, 1963 and for the record friends, I was not named after Dobie Gillis, the popular TV show character from the early 60s. I was actually named after Larry Doby, the Hall of Fame outfielder of the Cleveland Indians and the Jackie Robinson of the American League in baseball. My brother Larry also got his name from this man, whom my father, a baseball aficionado, admired. The spelling, however, is the same as the TV show character. The nurse at Cook County Hospital, where I was born, must have assumed I was named after Dobie Gillis and it's spelled that way on the birth certificate.

My baby sister Romona was born February 22, 1967, the year and month of the blizzard. We affectionately called her Mona and gave her the nickname Gator.

My Mother, born Estella Dale on October 18, 1926, is a short heavy-set woman with a smooth light brown complexion and a warm powerful voice. My "moms" is a homemaker, which is common for the times, and she is a most excellent one. She is a fantastic cook and everybody in the known world who ever tasted her cooking sure thought so. Our extended family always called on Stella to bake cakes and pies for them during the holidays.

My father, Curtis Holland was born on May 27, 1920. The son of sharecroppers, he was a short stocky dark-skinned man with strong hands. He was only five feet, seven inches tall, but he was a giant to me. He recently became jobless after working as a butcher for the

Swift meat packing company in the fabled Chicago Stockyards, because the company moved to Iowa.

My father chose to stay put in Chicago, even though the company offered to relocate us all. So twenty years of distinguished service were over and we lived on general assistance. We were poor by conventional standards, but we were never hungry and we always had nice things to wear and we had nice things around the house.

My daddy was not an educated man for most of his life, but he was learning to read and write at this point of his life. I liked sitting in his lap at night at his desk in he my mother's room and we would read together. His education became my salvation, because he educated me in the process. He would put on his black horn-rimmed specs and read me stories about sailing around the world and exploring the moon, which whet my appetite for adventure.

My father was a well-known and well-respected man in the neighborhood. He seemed to know everybody and everybody knew him. He was the precinct captain, which means he registered all the voters and supervised the elections in the area.

I would meet and shake hands with Mayor Richard J. Daley and Congressman Ralph Metcalfe—the Olympic Gold Medalist and Senator Paul Simon, known for his bow ties. I also got to meet Congressman Harold Washington, who would become the city's first elected black mayor in the 1980s. The Daley machine, as it was called by political pundits, was chugging along back in the day and his supporters (men like my father) were rewarded and his opponents were crushed like a cockroach under a boot.

I grew up in a very loving family and I had a fun and exciting childhood. My father was not big on public displays of affection, but I was a happy and well-adjusted child.

My mama had just whipped a feast big enough to feed an entire army on my birthday. She had a big yellow mixing bowl with her wooden spoon. She was making a German Chocolate cake just for me. She was also frying up a mess of fried chicken, while Dianne was peeling potatoes for the potato salad. Corn on the cob and other goodies were also on the menu.

She looked up from her cooking activities to glean me licking the big mixing spoon from the cake batter. My face had chocolate streaks across it. I rather enjoyed it.

"Look at you boy." You're a chocolate mess. Dianne, come and get Dobie and give him a bath."

Take a bath. You'll never take me alive. I scampered out of the kitchen like speedy scooter down the long corridor and turned left towards Rock, Jimmie and Leroy's room. Theirs was the most junkie room and I could smell old shoes and socks. There were three twin-sized beds line up military style against the back wall. There was a poster of Steve McQueen on a World War II motorcycle captured from his film the Great Escape and next to it was a poster of Clint Eastwood in his spaghetti Western Pancho snarling out at everyone like he does in the film, The Good, The Bad, And The Ugly. There was a huge window to the right and a huge closet to the left. The closet was full of discarded dry-cleaning plastic and hangers and clothes. So I opted to hide there under a nice pile of wintery clothes.

I didn't care much for sitting in a tub, getting scrubbed like a piece of dirty furniture or a filthy floor. My mama, wooh, she was the worst at it.

Although I felt I hid well, I was wrested from my hideout by a powerful hand—the hand of a butcher –with a firm grip around my ankle, I dangled in my father's grasp like a side of beef.

"C'mon on son, you're five now. You have to take your baths like a man," my father grumbled as he dragged me back to the bathroom where Dianne (thank God it's her and not my mother) was waiting and the water in the ivory tub was all ready drawn. She had the mildly amused big smile on her face.

My father returned me to the floor and he said, "I'll take you to Mr. Julius' shop after you bathe and dress. I think he has a birthday present for you." –Present. Well, why didn't you say so before, daddy. That was all he needed to say and I happily cooperated.

Dianne must have been working out, because she scrubbed my smooth brown skin with the washcloth rougher than ever. I endured the indignities of my scrubbing for a better cause and she wrapped my in a body-sized towel to dry off.

Dianne helped me dress in my blue jeans and white Snoopy t-shirt and my PF Fliers sneakers. My Snoopy T-shirt had a picture of the famous dog, lying on his back on top of his dog house with the caption bubble of "Happiness is a warm puppy" written on it.

As promised, my father delivered me to Mr. Julius' tailor shop on State Street just north of 55th street. Daddy would hold my hand and we would stroll down this path many times. We would pass the Mary C. Terrell Elementary School parking lot and then head south past the school and an assortment of shops—one of which being the B&B candy store and burger joint. Mr. and Mrs. Williams, the parents of my good friend Frankie, owned the B&B and they employed my brother Jimmie there as a short order cook and cashier. Frankie would later come to the birthday party. I was very fond of him. He was an only child, with lots of toys, but very few playmates. His home was atop the store and I believe I was the only one who could come over to play.

Mr. Julius' place was just a few doors down from the B&B. His shop was old and dimly lit and not very clean. The tile was worn away and all that remained was a sticky surface. There was a big well counter separating him from a bank of seats for customers. There were lots of sewing machines behind his counter and two large clothes pressing machines like you see in the cleaners. There were plastic runners that stretched from the entrance to the bank of seats.

Mr. Julius was a lot older than my father and he was a mulatto. He had thinning straight hair, which was always covered by his gray fedora hat, piercing blue eyes and the complexion of a white man. He used a brown mahogany cane to assist his walking. Mr. Julius supplied my father with pants and well-tailored suits, because back then, buying off the rack was still frowned upon by the old-timers. My father really seemed to like hanging out there shooting the breeze. I liked listening to the stories that my father and he and other men would exchange. Mostly they were stories about growing up black in the Jim Crow South, but Mr. Julius grew up in Chicago.

9

I never dared to ask his age but I think he was at least in his sixties, because he mentioned fighting in World War I. I think he needed the cane because he was injured in battle.

I remember him talking about the St. Valentine's Day Massacre—the famous gangland execution of North-Side gangsters in a garage in 1928. He also mentioned making a suit for old scar-face himself, Al Capone, when he was an up and coming gangster.

Mr. Julius was very fond of my father and me, but I got the impression that he didn't like kids very much. He wanted me to be his apprentice when I grew old enough to thread a needle and I considered it a great honor. The usual traffic that filled his shop was gone on this day, however. Mr. Julius was leaning on his cane with his right hand and pressing garments with the other when we walked in. He rarely smiled, but on this day he flashed a big dental-worked smile, with a missing bottom front tooth.

"Hello there. How are you old-timers today?"

"Fine, Mr. Julius, how are you," I said—because I was taught very young to speak to my elders and pay them respect, an art that has since died in our society, I'm afraid.

"I heard you were five years old today. "Man, you gettin' up there. I remember when you was a little baby and yo' daddy would bring you in a stroller. You was such a good baby. You never would cry."

I would blush now if it were possible. But instead I grinned from ear-to-ear.

"I told yo daddy he could bring you back anytime. And now, look at you. You's a big boy now. I hear you can read and carryin' on."

I nodded my head proudly.

Mr. Julius reached underneath the counter, leaning heavily on his cane, and handed me a box.

"Here ya go boy. Happy birthday, and many, many, more.

I beamed at the gold wrapping paper trying to glean what was inside.

"Go on. Open it," he motioned to me.

I looked at my father for permission. He nudged me with his approval and said, "go 'head."

I ripped the wrapping paper through the paper and it revealed a

10

lime-green hard cover book inside. It had lots of color pictures on the cover. I read the words and it said, P-I-C, P-I-C, T-I-O-N, Pictionary.

It had pictures of animals and household objects from A-to-Z. I love it, of course.

"OOOOOhhhh! Thank you! Thank you, Mr. Julius!

Awwhh, you welcome son." He smiled again.

"Well we better get on back home before you're late for your own party and yo mama ain't havin' that," my father said taking one of my hands off the book.

We said our cheerful goodbyes to Mr. Julius and my father said he would bring him back a slice of cake later. He waved us out the door and went back to pressing clothes.

The party rocked throughout the afternoon. Jimmie, dressed, in his gray knit shirt black slacks, had the deejay honors. He was spinning those hits on the hi-fi that got us up on the dance floor and shaking our booties. The living room furniture was moved into his room so that we would have a dance floor.

My boyhood buddies, Bruce and Gregory and Elton were there as well as my cousin Dennis. He came with my uncle Bill, my mom's youngest brother and his mother Cole Mae.

Curt brought his girlfriend Pam, who was very sweet on me and the feeling was mutual. She was the only woman that a naïve five-year-old who could kiss me on the jaw, without me wiping it off.

Rock and his best girl, Theresa, were there too. She gave the best hugs and of course I loved those. Rock and Theresa would later marry and have two sons, Sean and Dana.

The "Holland Five" made its debut by lip-synching to Smokey Robinson and the Miracles. Curt, Rock, Jimmie, Andrew, Larry were the leads. And for the first time they had a special guest crooner, me. We knew all their steps and all their moves from watching them perform on TV.

We all loved music, but none of us achieved great musical skill. Al had us watching all the old black and white musicals on television, such as Fred Astaire, Gene Kelly and Judy Garland; while Curt and Rock were into Motown—grooved to the Supremes, Stevie Wonder, Marvin Gaye, The Temptations and Smokey, of course.

Lottie's tastes exposed me to Aretha Franklin, Gladys Knight and the Pips, Billy Holiday and Dinah Washington; while Jimmie was a bit more alternative and dug tracks cut by Sly and the Family Stone, Ike and Tina Turner, the Fifth Dimension, and Jimmi Hendrix.

My father was the original old school dude, so when he played the tunes, they were from Nat King Cole, Ray Charles, B.B. King, James Brown and "Satchmo", Louis Armstrong.

My brother Rock had a 35-gallon aquarium on a meter-high metal stand. It had Angel Fish, and sea horses and colorful guppies galore. Today was the first day he let me feed them.

Andrew and Larry, went out to play after their performance with us as the "Holland Five". Dianne stayed around to assist my mother.

Curt and his monster mask made a special appearance to scare the living crap out of us. Curt was a world class Vincent Price—a real master of the macabre.

Rock's image of him holding up five fingers during the singing of happy birthday and the chorus asking, "how old are you". That image is forever etched in my mind.

Mona was sitting in her high chair, clapping and cheering as I blew out the five candles on my chocolate angel food cake. I blew out the candles with one breath so that my wish would come true. Funny thing though, I can't even remember what I wished for.

We had overdose levels of cake, ice cream, and hot dogs and potato chips and I can remember feeling so full that I thought my little belly would burst. I think everyone had a great time—I know I did—and they all left the party smiling as the sun prepared to set.

My big brothers put the furniture back in the living room and went with their girlfriends as we "youngins" sat in front of the TV set to watch some prime time programming. "Bewitched," starring Elizabeth Montgomery and Dick York, was the intended TV viewing. They were a loving suburban couple, who happened to be magical, particularly the missus.

12

But on the night of my fifth birthday, the opening credits failed to roll, because the program was interrupted by a special news bulletin. David Brinkley announced with a heavy heart that the Reverend Dr. Martin Luther King Jr. was shot and fatally wounded as he stood on the balcony with colleagues at the Lorraine Motel in Memphis, Tennessee.

At the time, I really didn't know Dr. King and his impact on our society, but I knew it was not good when anybody was killed. My parents retired to their bedroom to grieve in private, I think. We sat there in silence and shock and awe... Happy Birthday to me.

Chapter 2
Las Vegas Vervain

Troy had just gulped his eighteenth cup of coffee. His eyes were bulging out of the sockets; sweat rolled down his coffee colored brow, his throat was dry from caffeine saturation. No way, however, would he put an end to his frenzy now. He was on a roll and out of control—a picture of calm on the outside.

"Put it all on 32 black," he said, trying to evoke his best Sean Connery.

As the roulette wheel spun and the white ball danced around it, making a clip-ity-clap sound, the gathering crowd held its collective breath, spellbound without as much as a sound.

Troy got that feeling again. It was the same feeling he had 12 hours ago when his odyssey began at the craps table. It was the same feeling he had at the black jack table. It was the feeling he had at the slot machines. He also had this feeling at keno. He had to pee. He had to piss like the proverbial racehorse. He had to piss like the mobster obsessed with carrying out a vendetta. He was committed only to that need for the time being.

"Thirty-two black" the croupier said. It was more like a sigh of disbelief. Troy was baffled as well, particularly because he was sure he would lose this time. People in "Sin City" always did — lose that is.

The onlookers erupted into cheers as if they were watching the Super Bowl and their team had scored a mind-blowing spectacular touchdown. The astonished croupier dished out more cash to the jittery black man, who by some mind-altering state of affairs was un-phased by his largess.

15

"Cash it all in," he said calm, cool and collected, as he breathed in deeply he could smell the expensive colognes and perfumes and he felt a rush of fear and doubt well-up in his bosom. Two barrel-chested security guards in black tailored suits escorted him away from the table. The adoring crowd congratulated him as he walked out, patting him on the back—grateful to bear witness to the greatest win-streak they would probably ever see.

Troy had only one thing on his mind and so he promptly sprinted for the nearest toilet, the male one of course; stood at the urinal, unzipped his fly and let loose with the most blissful piss he had ever experienced—at least in the last two hours.

"Ahhhhhh," he let out with most emotion he had shown in hours. And, why not? It was a difficult set of circumstances that led him here and all the stress balls and yoga in the wide world of sports couldn't alleviate his burden. Nothing could do that, but the outpouring from his little brother was a start. Let's start at the beginning...

It was a Monday morning in Cleveland, Ohio.

Troy Davis is his name and he is the newest sports columnist for the Cleveland Plain Dealer. Troy had acquired the habit of waking bright and early and this morning was no exception. He's writing an inspired piece about the Cleveland Indians baseball team. He didn't try to show it, but the pressure of his new-found responsibilities was getting to him. It was a promotion and yet he wasn't sleeping well. He wasn't eating well. Not to mention his loss of appetite for some of life's other pleasures—his college sweetheart and live-in girlfriend, Gina, could attest to that. But this morning she was going to put a spice up their morning if it killed them.

Troy sat on the corner of their bed in only his boxers, hunched over his lap top—a newer more sophisticated model than the one he had when he was just a beat writer. Gina stepped through the connecting bathroom door, whisks of hot steam in her wake. She had the look of determination in her eyes and she was pulling out a few of her tools of seduction. For one, she was wearing only a blue terry-clothed towel that Troy admired her in most. And secondly, she was wearing nothing else.

Troy, however, known for his keen observation and insight as a reporter, failed miserably in noticing his beautiful lady's sinews as she stood seductively in front of him. It was a disturbing trend that had grown more frequent of late and Gina was worried that if she didn't take charge, her love of her life could be lost.

So her plan was to get him hot and bothered or bothered then hot so he would rip that towel off her; and they would make the kind of love that made their neighbors rife with envy, when they passed each other in the corridors of their Shaker Heights apartment. She would go to work happy and he would write with renewed vigor.

"Troy," she let it in low throaty tone.

But he continued to press the keys of his new computer.

"Troy," she said louder and obviously annoyed this time.

Still no response from Troy though.

"Troy", she said louder and more forcefully.

"Hmmm?" but he didn't dare look up.

"Troy," she shouted, finally snapping the interface between man and machine.

"Do you like what you see?" she said smiling seductively.

He glared at her with new eyes—first, not seeing her in complete focus. Then he noticed her melon-sized breasts, with protruding nipples, heaving at him through the towel. Her curvaceous hips and narrow waste made her damn sexy. Her chocolate brown runner's thighs and feminine meaty calves dripped ever so lightly with droplets of water that her smooth skin glistens. Her short hair, which was not quite combed and a bit damp, gave her an added quality of a seductress.

Troy, who is twenty-nine years old and far from dead, pushed aside his computer box and rose from the bed so that he was in front of his lady love.

"What do we have here!" he smiled.

He palmed a handful of breast through the towel and Gina pushed them into his grasp to excite him even more. Then he removed the towel from her in a motion that a magician trick.

17

You know the old removing-a-table-cloth-without-disturbing-the-flowers-on-the-table-trick.

"Voilá," he said. "The mounds of eternal joy."

"And for my next trick," he said removing his boxers. "An exploration of the caverns of love."

"You're so silly." She giggled but she was totally turned on by his aroused body.

He kissed her gently between her breasts and his thick full lips delicately worked their way down to those caverns. Gina moaned and groaned and she grabbed him by his woolen-haired head in appreciation of Troy's long and powerful tongue as it bathed her with affection and appreciation. He wrapped his arms around her waist and hoisted her into the air before gently placing her on the bed underneath him.

"So you want to play nasty baby?"

"Uh-huh," she said, barely able to respond through her pants of passion. In his best dirty Al Pacino in Scarface Cuban accent, he said, "Let me introduce you to my lil friend."

"A modest man is very sexy, you know."

She arched her back in anticipation of his impending entry. But Troy teased her crowning glory a bit, rubbing his member along the outskirts of the rich and fertile fields of love. Gina squirmed and squealed in delight because only Troy had mastered how to push her to ecstatic heights. But she couldn't stand it for long so she wrapped her arms around his neck and pulled him down so that he slid right inside her.

"This is where I belong. Right here. Right now, with the finest woman in the land, making sweet love. Conjuring up the Lord.

They laughed.

The love-making session was short but very satisfying for Gina had to get to work. Troy was still naked, as she showered again and dressed, writing his column. She came over to the bed so he could kiss her good-bye, when the phone rang. He dove across the bed for the phone, leaving Gina in full pucker.

"Hello, Stan. I've been expecting your call."

18

Gina was still frozen in a pucker when she straightened up to think 'Well, dissed by him for the office again.' She left the apartment without her goodbye kiss. Troy tried to catch her but she was all ready out the door.

"Well my man. What are you going to send us today," Stan Cox, the sports editor of the Plain Dealer said into his raised hand phone.

"I'm sending the column about the Indian's chances of winning the pennant this year. I am so psyched about their chances actually. The Tribe will be great in 1998," they chuckled.

"I look forward to reading it Troy.

Cox, a veteran of the newspaper for twenty-eight years, knew better than his young and enthusiastic colleague. He knew that the Indians had not made it to the World Series since 1954, when Hall of Fame shortstop and player manager Lou Boudreaux, and fellow Hall of Fame pitcher Bob Lemon and Hall of Fame outfielder Larry Doby suited up for the team recently plagued by defeat.

The Indians have had some success in the 90s, making the playoffs, but have been eliminated by their hated rivals, the New York Yankees before making it to the World Series in 1997 and losing to the Florida Marlins. Cox, who characterizes himself as an optimistic cynic, Troy would have to be very convincing to persuade him and the downtrodden fans plagued by defeat and desperation.

"Oh by the way kiddo: Doc's illness is going to keep him on the shelf a bit longer than expected and I need you to cover for him on the big fight in Las Vegas this weekend.

"Me? Are you sure?"

"That's right buddy. This is a big time opportunity for you, you know."

"Sure I do and I will do the job Stan, like I always do."

"Great. So I can count on you."

"You know it Stan."

"Fantastic. You leave for Vegas tomorrow."

"Tomorrow! Shit Stan. Gina and I were going to Hilton Head on my days off. You know, Tuesday and Wednesday. She has been looking forward to this so much. Hell, she even gave me some this morning."

"No problem, Troy"…Stan seemed to be thinking. "I'll give Danny Dixon a crack at it. Far be it from me to stand between a man and his love of nooky."

"No!" Troy was shocked at how loudly and quickly the word flew out of his mouth. He was not willing to give way to his fiercest rival in the sports department—the man he narrowly beat out for the position he now holds on too tightly.

"No Stan," this time he said it more controlled. "I'll explain it to her."

"You sure, buddy," Stan could barely hold back his smile.

"Yeah, I'm sure," but Troy was not smiling.

"Take her out some place nice and crowded. That way she won't make a scene. And lay a nice gift on her."

"Thanks Stan, but Gina's not the kind of girl you can buy off with trinkets."

"My boy, you can buy them all off with trinkets."

"Man, no wonder you're on your third divorce," Troy regretted saying that, really.

But Stan took it in stride and chuckled a deep-throated laugh of enjoyment.

"Well, you handle it your way. You young folks today, with your new fangled ideas like 'may I touch you there?'"

"Any who, I'll have your flight tickets delivered by messenger before three this afternoon. Good luck, Troy."

And Stan hung up the phone before Troy could say thank you.

"I'm gonna need it."

Lady luck was not on his side when he broke the news to Gina and now he was on his way to do a job, which he questioned doing since the reason he decided to do it—which was to make a better life for woman he wanted to marry—was now out of the picture. Troy had sunk to an all-time new low. If image was worth anything in monetary value, Troy Davis of Chicago, Illinois, was flat broke, busted, penniless. In the board game Monopoly, they say 'do not pass go. Do not collect two hundred dollars.' Perhaps more appropriately for his sports writing genre, 'game, set and match by the score of six-love, six-love.'

Troy's eyes glazed over like he was in a catatonic state, but some way, somehow he managed to walk aimlessly as he disembarked from the plane in Las Vegas on a Wednesday afternoon. He hardly noticed the pretty flight attendant flirting with him. He didn't notice when the captain asked everyone to look at the Hoover Dam. He didn't notice the slot machines blinking and the curvy women dressed in tight-fitting cat suits as he drifted through the airport.

Troy nearly walked away with some other guy's luggage at the baggage claim, before the actual owner intervened. He got his bag and drifted outside to the curb for a cab, but he didn't notice the attendant asking him if he need a ride.

"Sir! Do you need a cab! A bearded man shouted with an Indian accent.

Troy snapped out of his trance. The traffic, noise and smell of gas fumes surrounded him like a wave of emotion to his senses.

Troy opened his mouth to speak.

"Hey Troy," a voice from a passing car must have shouted his name.

He craned his neck for a better look and recognized the culprit as none other than his old friend, Terry Jones.

"Terry," he shouted back, surprising the taxi attendant with the life in his voice. "What's up cuz."

"I won't be needing that cab," he told the Indian attendant. Whose eyes were wide with amazement.

Troy hoisted his bag more enthusiastically and headed for a red Ford Mustang that Terry was driving. Once he got inside, he saw his friend with new eyes. He could see his bright white smile. His big brown eyes—his goatee and his tremendously dark muscled biceps sticking out of a t-shirt so he held out his hand open palmed for a soul brother handshake and Troy smiled bright and wide for the first time. Terry toggled the five-speed stick to put the car in drive and off they motored onto the highway.

"So what's good brotha? You were looking like you lost your best friend back there. It's a good thing you found me," he flashed those brilliant teeth again.

Troy laughed hard and that had not happened in about twelve hours as well.

Then it dawned on him again. "Well, Terry I did. Gina and I broke up."

There was an awkward pause from Troy, who began to realize his college friend and roommate was not joking.

"So what happened?"

Troy shrugged his broad shoulders limply.

"You know how it goes, man—all work and no play… I love you but…blah blah blah.

"Wow! I can't believe that bro. You two were my best hope for all poor slobs who still believed there was a babe for us out there. Now—"

Terry decided not to use that last sentence. It would have done more harm than good he figured.

"Shocking. Positively shocking," he mimicked Sean Connery.

Terry turned to look at him, but Troy stared blankly at the bluffs. There was a road sign, indicating they were five miles away from the city limits of Las Vegas.

"Let me buy you a drink, man," he said jokingly, because Troy was a teetotaler. When they were in college, Terry and their buddies used to tease Troy—questioning whether or not he was really from Chicago—because he didn't party like a Chicagoan should.

"Thanks Terry, I could use a drink, bruh."

Terry nearly lost control of the wheel. He faced Troy with eyes of absolute astonishment.

They drove into the gigantic circular drive of the MGM Grand Hotel. The fountains spraying a cooling mist when the stepped out of the sports car. The MGM Grand would be the venue for the upcoming championship bout, more specifically—the giant tent-like structure behind the hotel—the MGM Grand Gardens Casino.

Troy ordered a Scotch on the rocks with a beer chaser and Terry had to raise an eyebrow in disbelief. He looked around the brightly lit bar which had no windows, but plenty of slot machines and noise to go with it and said," Make that two."

Terry had been with the San Francisco Chronicle newspaper for a year, after spending five years with the Miami Herald and two years with the Atlanta Journal Constitution, but he was from Los Angeles. They first met a freshman mixer at Northwestern University in Chicago. Terry was a junior who had landed an impressive internship with the Chicago Tribune and he was asked to find some young African American journalists to mentor and guide through the awesome journalism program at NU. He heard about Troy from a few of professors and when they met, he immediately took a liking to this bashful but eloquent "freshie."

They became roommates Troy's sophomore year, when he met Gina. Terry would give him advice on how to romance her but Gina was not a big fan of Terry's. So when Terry graduated he went to grad school and Troy and Gina have been roommates ever since. Terry and Troy remained in touch and when Troy went to Grad school, Terry would take him on assignments with him while he was working in Atlanta.

When Troy landed in Cleveland two years ago, Gina happily followed her man. And Terry was on the phone first to congratulate his "little bro." Now Terry was the first one to learn his bad news about his relationship.

That one drink had knocked a novice like Troy for a loop, however. And Terry had to drive his wobbly friend to his hotel.

"Where ya stayin' Troy."

"Ah, I don't know I don't won't to stay in that apartment without Gina.

Terry shook his head. This is even worse than he had anticipated.

"I mean, in Las Vegas, where are you stayin'?

Ahh…. Ahhh Da Marriott Sweeeeets!"

Terry tried to be level-headed.

"You can't gamble there. Them Mormons won't allow it!

"I koooooooowwwww! Was Troy's drunken reply.

The valet fetched Terry's car and he tipped him five bucks and they helped stuff Troy into the passenger seat. Terry spun out

23

the drive like an expectant father with his pregnant wife. The car hummed down Vegas Boulevard a block west to Paradise Drive. It was about a couple of miles from the Strip to the Marriott Suites. Terry pulled up to the curb of the Suites and gave Troy a-once-over.

"Are you going to be okay?

Ya man, don't worry about little ole me. I'm a big boy now. Troy made a mock salute with his right hand and got out of the car.

"Don't forget the press briefing and dinner tonight at nine o'clock. Should I pick you up?

Troy pirouetted around to face his friend. "Naw, I'll meet you there, it's no problem. I can walk it even.

Terry and Troy were different people and yet, they were two African American males who enjoyed a good sports story. In that regard they were kindred spirits. Blacks were not always able to do these jobs in the past and so it was uncommon for other blacks to get together and show each other how it was done.

They were both excellent reporters and very creative writers, however. Terry, when he was the beat writer for the Miami Heat, wrote some fantastic stories for the Herald. Here's a sample of one of those stories he wrote:

MIAMI—Gong! Gong! Gong! Do not ask for whom the bell tolls Miami Heat fans, for it tolls for thee and any hopes and dreams of winning its first NBA Championship along with it.
After a spectacular 50-win season and a magical tour of the world's toughest league, the Heat saw their fiery success story disappear in a puff of smoke in the first round of the playoffs, courtesy of those hated rivals the New York Knicks.

Troy was just as inventive with his stories. He wrote this on after the Cleveland Indians lost the American League Championship Series in baseball to its arch-rivals the New York Yankees.

New York—Once again those "Damn Yankees" tapped-danced across our *Indians and home plate more times than dancers in a Bob Fosse musical.*
The Cleveland Indians' debut on the Great White Way received

24

poor reviews as the defending World Champions notched a 15-2 victory.

Some of the Yankees even dazzled the 52,000 screaming and jeering Yankee Stadium fans with curtain calls. Enter Bernie Williams. The Yankees' center-fielder drove in five runs on four hits, including a long towering grand slam home run to deep center field more than 440 monstrous feet from home plate.

The warm Nevada sun was preparing to rest on the other city in America that never sleeps, Las Vegas. Vegas is home of the famous hotel New York, New York which is a mini replica of the Big Apple, New York City. Bright multi-colored neon lights flickered and sparkled in the galaxy in the desert to wink in another busy night.

Troy stepped out of the shower at 8 p.m. feeling a bit heavy headed and still heavy hearted as he prepared to dress for the media banquet.

He slipped on his Major League Baseball boxer shorts, the ones with the logos of all the baseball teams on them and his lucky t-shirt with the logo of his favorite band in college, Fishbone. The logo is just that, a fish's bone with a circle around it and the words "Fuck Racism" underneath.

He surprised himself how nimble he felt though. He hopped into a pair of blue khaki pants and pulled on a blue Hawaiian shirt over it and a pair of Birkenstock shoe sandals with white socks.

The month of February in the desert oasis was warmer than usual. It was a balmy eighty-four degrees in the day time and a very comfortable sixty-four degrees at night. Troy had just come from a winter wonderland in Cleveland. So it felt like the middle of July to him.

Thoughts of Gina had begun to permeate his mood. She had bought him the Drakar Noir cologne he splashed on himself liberally. And she picked out the chronographic watch he strapped on his wrist. Hell, he kissed Gina for the first time, while wearing that Fishbone t-shirt, which is why he believed it to be lucky.

He decided to get out of the room and into the fresh air. He stood outside in front of his hotel and breathed in the cool night air deeply into his lungs. Wisps of breath could be seen coming out of his mouth. He walked east towards the bright lights of the Mirage Hotel on the Strip, which he could see the neon sign from a distance. The weather was absolutely gorgeous for an evening stroll and Troy decided to do just that.

The Strip was teeming with hundreds—no thousands of pedestrians at 9 p.m. He compared it to Cleveland and figured downtown Cleveland would be winding down at this time. The entryway to the 5,000-room MGM Grand was a majestic half-mile long semi-circle drive up. Troy stepped into the lobby and the décor was kindred to the Emerald Palace from the Wizard of Oz—plush green carpet and golden walls stretched through a massive temple or cathedral.

He saw the sign for the press gathering near the front desk and walked towards it looking for his friend. He arrived on foot with not a minute to spare. But in a place with thousands of people from all walks of life, Terry did not stick out in the crowd. There was a constant and random pinging and ringing and ponging sounds from slot machines serving as a reminder of what this town is really known for. As he reached the lobby desk, he spotted Terry—looking chilled back in a pair of Bermuda shorts and an oversized polo shirt. He was in a pair of blue suede Adidas sneakers and ankle-high white socks.

They clasped hands by the thumb and half-hugged each other and marched through the lobby into the Convention Center. They were greeted there by a couple of thick-necked security guards who were dressed green jackets and gold slacks and white oxford collarless shirts. The guards checked the names on their press credentials they wore chained around their necks. They asked them to wear the placard credentials at all times but it sounded more like a command.

The banquet hall was kindred to a giant cave. There were scores of large round dining tables in rows, leading up to the stage where the podium and speakers' tables were. There were still a few tables near the podium and they sat there. Media members from all around the world were present. The press has a very good since of humor and they passed the time telling war stories with funny endings.

Terry went over near the bar in the back of the room and chatted with a half-dozen guys from New York, Troy heard them say. But he wasn't feeling very chatty himself so he drifted away. His mind began to wander, mostly it landed on thoughts of Gina—how she wanted to come here for their honeymoon and how she would like being here now.

He realized with each passing moment just how much she had become a part of his life. What would the odds be of him ever getting over her? The odds-makers would never take that bet—not even in Vegas.

Troy's spirits plummeted like the hotel's speedy elevator. Not even boxing promoter Don King's wild hairdo could lift his spirits. He attempted to focus on the spectacle at hand, but he just couldn't do it. When Puerto Rican boxer Felix Trinidad came in to say hello (speaking mainly in Spanish through a translator), Troy was nearly in tears.

Terry made a joke about Don King's hair to snap Troy out of his funk, but he knew his friend was in a downward spiral. Terry said a prayer to himself, "Lord, give my friend Troy the strength to get through this."

Ding....

The opening bell ushered in the main event, finally. After two lesser-known sets of fighters beat the holy hell out of each other and a pair of women pummeled each other, the main event had commenced.

The Golden Boy as Oscar de la Hoya is called, prepared to do battle with Felix "The Silent Assassin" Trinidad. Both fighters were undefeated and both were Olympic gold medalists. De la Hoya, a Mexican American, had plenty of fans across the border swooning for his baby-faced good looks.

Trinidad, from Puerto Rico, was a low-key fighter, who shunned the bright lights of the game. He would let his powerful jab and knee bending combinations speak for him in the ring. In his previous fight, he completely mangled top-notched champion Fernando Vargas, another great Mexican American fighter.

Troy snapped out of his haze long enough to pay attention to this fight, because it was too good not to. Earlier that week, he put two hundred dollars down at one of the book maker shops for his editor Stan on De la Hoya, who was heavily favored. But Troy, liking Trinidad's demeanor and three-to-one odds, bet on ole Felix. He put a thousand of his hard earned dollars down—the money he was saving to buy Gina's engagement ring. He figured it would be a symbolic way of letting go of a love that once bloomed.

Troy had two sleepless nights in Vegas and he began to feel the effects so he ordered a cup of coffee with cream and two sugars during the fifth round of the fight.

It was a rich and aromatic Kenyan blend they served with Irish Crème creamer and raw rock sugar that Troy found quite delicious. He ordered several more cups throughout the fight—which went the distance, by the way.

The twelve-round battle of these two welterweight Titans ended with Trinidad winning a unanimous decision. He would have loved to have seen the look on Stanley Cox's face, when he realized he lost two hundred bucks. But Troy had won. He had won. Oh no, he had won and his one thousand dollars had multiplied into three.

A surge of energy coursed through Troy's veins, probably from the coffee and he needed to file his story, which went like this:

LAS VEGAS— *The city with more excitement in its bathrooms than most places, just got a little bit more exciting. The odds-makers here went cuckoo as two undefeated champions slugged it out, all 140-pounds of them. But in the end, Oscar De La Hoya, went home empty handed because Felix Trinidad had won a thrilling unanimous 12-round decision.*
The 10,000 faithful at the MGM Grand Gardens Casino roared with disappointment that reverberated as far south as the tip of Mexico. And the crowd also thunder-clapped with resounding

28

approval that may be heard as far south east as San Juan, where they must certainly be dancing in the streets to celebrate the biggest victory of the career of Puerto Rico's favorite son...

Troy had just won three thousand dollars and wasn't happy. He felt that he had just tripled his burden. The time was nearly 1 a.m. and he was racing. His palms were clammy and his pulse was, well, racing. So he raced with his winnings to the nearest hotel, Caesar's Palace to get rid of his largess.

Prior to his visit to the Palace, he chatted a bit with Terry. Terry told how he dropped three hundred bucks. He didn't want to tell him how much he just won. They talked something about the fight, but he really couldn't remember exactly what and Terry said goodbye. He was driving back to L.A. that night and he wanted to get home and enjoy his days off.

The slot machines in Caesar's were jingling with disappointment really and Troy had hoped to cash out with the other losers. But he figured the roulette tables would be quicker.

Troy put three thousand down on the plush roulette surface and hoped for a merciful end to his suffering. He put the money on the number 16, because it was Gina's birth date.

The croupier didn't blink at his lofty bet. Instead he asked if everyone could check their bets before he let fly with the wheel. The ball on the roulette wheel danced around for what seemed like an eternity.

"Sixteen- red," he announced professionally. Damn, he won.

The people were all ecstatic. A silver-haired man with a young busty blond shouted at him. "Way to go son!"

The croupier, whose name was Bart, but he had on his co-worker Larry's name tag. It's a long story but the part-time Elvis imper-sonator had to make a fast get-a-way and left his uniform behind.

"Check your bets people," Bart, Larry spoke with more feeling as he spun the wheel.

Troy put his money this time on 32 because it was twice as much as 16. He ordered more coffee from a scantily clad waitress.

"32, we have a winner," said Bart-Larry.

29

The blond woman let out a yelp of astonishment and exultation. But Troy was not impressed and neither was the croupier.

"Let it ride."

Everyone at the table shouted. A group of passersby stopped to witness the commotion as well.

Bart-Larry, sensing the moment, also decided to seize the moment and he let the wheel fly like Elvis pointing off stage.

The wheel ran round and round and Troy seemed unfazed. He knew something that the others didn't. He wanted to lose and he would be damned if he didn't do it faster.

"32". That's all Bart-Larry could say.

Now everyone around the table seemed impressed and others from the table were gathering around to watch Troy. His coffee arrived and he took a huge gulp and said: "One more time Larry."

The crowd grasped. They couldn't believe it. There was a smell of excitement around the table.

He drank down his cup of coffee before Bart-Larry could say it. Those words he was hoping to hear.

"I don't BELIEVE IT—32!!!

Uggghhh!!!! Was Troy's reaction.

Maybe I'll try something else. So he cashed it in. A short baby-faced Asian man with bushy hair walked up to him and smiled his approval.

Troy couldn't believe it. He had won. But he had to pee. He scurried to the nearest toilet with pockets filled with cash. As he relieved himself at the urinal, the emotions poured out. A tear trickled out of his left eye. It was just like the night Gina left. Up until now, the break up itself had managed not to enter his consciousness. But now they came flooding back…

Troy and Gina were in the cozy window booth of Sartie's,
a popular night spot in Shaker Heights. Gina never looked lovelier than she did that night. She wore a kente´ cloth head band around her shortly cropped afro and a black turtle neck sweater that clung to her breasts. She wore skin-tight designer jeans and black platform

shoes. She was the retro-poster child for sexy ladies everywhere.

He felt mad love for her—even more so tonight—because he sensed what could be at stake and he was proud to be seen in public with her. Sweat rolled down his temples and his hands were sweating. Their plans to go to Hilton Head if handled wrong could blow up in his face. He had a plan but he was reconsidering as Gina sat there looking like the love of his life. He figured that honesty would be the best road, because that's what she valued most.

He looked Gina in the eye, took her by the hand and said, "you're the most beautiful woman in the building, as always. I can't believe how lucky I am every time I wake up next to you."

Gina's smile went to a frown. "What's, wrong baby? You've been somewhere else all night. Is it work?

The busboy came to the table with chips and salsa and placed them on the center of the table. He placed a clear glass filled with ice water in front of each of them. Troy thanked the fresh-faced Latino and he disappeared into the background of the restaurant. People were laughing and rocking back and forth in their seats to the soulful sounds of Motown.

Troy gulped down a few swallows of ice-water, hoping it would moisten his parched throat.

"Stan wants me to go to Las Vegas to cover the big fight this weekend."

"Troy, that's wonderful. I'm so happy for you," she paused and thought about for a moment. "When do you leave?"

Her tone was sharper now.

"Tomorrow morning," he dropped his lower lip to expose a row of perfect bottom teeth.

"Oh I see. No wonder you were so worried."

He looked down at the table.

"How on earth did Stan twist your arm on this one?

She scowled a bit looking through him when he finally lifted his gaze to face hers. No words came out of his mouth, however.

"Oh, I know. He said it would further your career. Don't you know you've gone about as far as you can go here babe. It's all I hear lately.

31

She started waving her arms in the air. "My career. My career. My damn precious career.

He felt shame and guilt and impotence.

"Babe, I don't ask much of you but I have to tell you—

A long-haired brunette waitress appeared in front of them. She was about to ask if they were ready to order, but she sensed the tension.

"I'll give you folks a few more minutes," she retreated to the back.

"I have to tell you," Gina continued. "I think you love your job more than me." She looked guilty for saying it but it was something she just had to say.

"Now you know that's just not true, muffin. You are my queen. My Venus and your love inspires me to do whatever it takes. Sometimes that means to kiss Stan Cox's ass," Troy had found his voice.

"That may be true. But I think you found a new lover that even I can't compete with and she is a demanding bitch that takes you away from home, keeps you out all hours and makes you break your promises."

"This is just temporary, now that I have a column—

"That's just it. You have a column. Your ass-kissing days should be over. Let them use some other wannabe."

"Things will get better—I promise; and I will make it up to you, Gina. Please try to understand baby, please."

"Troy, I do understand. That's the problem. I understand the problem better than you do, because you can't see it as a problem."

Troy's head snapped back like he received a stiff jab to the face.

"I've lived through this before with my mother and my father. It's not your fault. You're just trying to be a good man and provide for us. If anyone is to blame, it's me. Because I let it go on this far because I'm in love with you and I would do anything for you. It's going to be so hard living without you"—

"You're leaving me?"

He sighed and tears welled up in his eyes. He was stunned beyond comprehension. His chest caved in and he could hardly breathe. He looked away to gather his composure and he let go of her hand. He missed her touch all ready. A tear began to stream down his cheek, but he wiped it away.

"Okay then. If that's how you want it, I'll get my stuff out when I get back from Vegas."

He had hoped he could talk his way back in after they spent some time apart.

"You can do that, but I won't be there when you get back. I'm going back to Chicago and get on with my life. You know, I have dreams I want to accomplish too and in case you haven't noticed, I can't accomplish them here."

Troy rocked back in the booth again. He was KO'ed.

"I am so sorry Troy for doing this so suddenly but I've been wooed by a few universities back there and I know this is the best for both of us. I know you love me like no man ever loved me before.

"But," and she shook her head in disbelief when she said this, "it's not enough."

She caressed his face ever so gently, and said, "Good-bye my love. Have a safe trip."

She rose from the table and left the restaurant without looking back. Troy was shocked and he couldn't move, because he wanted to go after her.

"Damn."

That's all he could muster and he said that under his breath...

Troy's win-streak was more amazing than the Los Angeles Lakers 35-game win streak back in the 70s. The craps tables at the Grand paid off. The money wheel at Treasure Island paid even more money. He could get no satisfaction or relief of his burden, which had bulged to a whopping two-hundred and thirty thousand dollars. The only relief was his strange affiliation with the bean—coffee, java, or joe.

It was five in the morning and he was more wired than a speed freak at a rave party. He made his way to the Riviera, where he started to make some headway by losing. He was losing ten thousand dollars a pop at their big money slots. Lady luck, however, had discovered him again. A nice neat row of Golden sevens lined up for him. Jackpot, again! Damn! Add seven seventy thousand more to the pot.

Two middle-aged heavy-set Black women were nearby when they saw him ring in the good luck. The women were visiting with a church group from Compton and they were ecstatic for Troy. One dark-skinned lady hugged him so tight, he couldn't breathe. The fairer-skinned one kissed him on the jaw, leaving a nice lipstick mark on it.

"Congratulations, sugah." They both shouted

Troy went limp in the woman's arms and he managed to escape her grasp.

"God in Heaven!!!"

The women shouted back, "Yes baby, the Lord has sho' blessed you!"

"Yes indeed chile," the dark woman said.

Troy buried his face in his hands. By this time a sharply dressed woman with short black hair had appeared. She escorted him to claim his prize, because contrary to popular belief, that much money doesn't come out the slot machine.

Troy was overwhelmed, but he finally had an idea.

"Oh no, it's not me. These ladies won the prize." He waved towards the two ladies like he was a game show host.

The sharp dressed woman looked surprised but she went along with it.

The heavy ladies screamed and shouted hysterically as they jumped up and down hugging each other. They tried to hug Troy but he was well on his way to the exit.

Troy was clenching his teeth wondering how to dispense of this blasted money. There was a pre-dawn chill in the air and he could see his breath as he breathed in heavily. He walked a rapid pace across the street and into Circus Circus Hotel. A huge circus tent draped the entrance of the tall and wide building.

He bounced into Circus Circus, feeling dizzy and a bit disoriented. The shock and the stress and the coffee jolts had put his system into overload. He looked up at the ceiling and the crystal chandelier at the top of the big tent began to spin around. Troy Davis collapsed like a cheap card table flat on his back.

Most people ignored him and continued gambling, while others went to check on him. A few staff people and security came over to check on him.

Troy was delirious and kept muttering: "I'm a fool. I'm a fool."

Then he slipped out of consciousness…

Troy awoke in a strange white room. His vision was blurred, but he could hear two men standing near his bed talking quietly. The man on the right did not look familiar. He wore a white coat. The other man looked vaguely familiar—the 6-foot frame and dark curly hair and the long pointy nose. It was none other than his editor, Stanley Cox.

Troy wanted to sit up and tell Stan to get the hell out of his room, but his head had church bells ringing in it. So he moaned and rested back into his pillow.

The two men heard his moaning and came over to check on him. The other man was a shorter Indian man with a very handsome face and long wavy black hair. He was a doctor for the hotel. The staff brought him to their infirmary when they saw all the cash on him. So security locked his dough away in a safe deposit box and called the house doctor to take care of him. Later, they moved him into a suite. The staff checked his ID and found his credentials and called the Plain Dealer.

Stan actually flew out on the first thing he could book. Troy was actually touched by the sentiment. It was now Monday morning and he was unconscious for nearly a day.

The doctor left the room so they could talk alone.

"So you're still alive. Just what the hell were you trying to do my man? Kill yourself. You actually overdosed on caffeine. I didn't know that was even possible. You know you're no good to us if you're dead Troy."

Troy felt anger pouring over him and the bells were subsiding.

"Yeah, no thanks to you"

35

That hurt more than he expected. So he cupped his forehead.

"Where is this hostility coming from? You're my guy Troy. Don't I take care of you?"

"Gina left me over this trip."

"Oh no, Troy. I am so sorry. But that's life my man. Why do you think I have been married three times."

Stan paced to the other side of Troy's bed and opened the curtain, letting in bright sun light, through tented glass. But they both had to squint.

"Doctor's orders, I'm afraid."

Cox walked back to the other side of the room.

"If you love her sooo much Troy. You have to fight for her. Don't go out and kill yourself on some binge. You have no chance if you're dead."

The room was dead silent. Stan always knew what to say to inspire Troy. He was the Phil Jackson to Troy's Michael Jordan, a true Zen Master of minds.

"Stan, you're right."

"I know am buddy."

"I'm going back to Chicago and I hope that Gina will take me back."

"Good idea. Take all the time you need and when you get back, we'll be ready to rock and roll again."

"If Gina takes me back, I'm not coming back Stan."

Woh buddy. Let's not be hasty, here Troy. That's a knee-jerk reaction. What I like about you is that you always think things through."

"I didn't. I thought things through because I was indecisive and weak. I need her Stan. I need her to complete me. She is my rock. I was strong when I was with her and I could stand myself more. Now I can't. I just pray to God she takes me back."

Troy got out of bed and was feeling stronger all ready as he went to the closet and put on his clothes.

"I see. You were one of the best writers I ever knew. You could have been one of the greats—like Grantland Rice or Frank DeFord or Wendell Smith or me.

They laughed.

"I'm just a guy in love and I like that better than anything. Thanks for everything Stan. I mean that."

They shook hands. Stan walked out of the room still surprised by what had transpired.

Troy had come to his senses so he picked up his winnings and dropped by Cartier's jewelry store. He bought s three-carat rock and he hoped maybe Gina would succumb to really big trinkets. Then he placed one more bet. He bet twenty grand on the New Yankees to win the World Series at three to one odds. Then he went on to Chicago.

Troy showed up at Gina's mother's house that night with flowers in one hand and diamond wedding ring in the other hand and on one knee asked her to marry him. She agreed, of course.

"But there's gonna be changes around here."

One more thing—the Yankees, they won the World Series, again....

Chapter 3

The Class of '69

April 1969: Off to the races...

I leapt out of bed in my Major League Baseball logo pajamas, sprinted into the living room and pulled the switch on our Zenith floor model 26-inch black and white television. Nowadays this would be considered an odd size for a floor model television set, but in 1969 it was state-of-the-art. The TV stood on four legs with an outward bulging picture tube face and a big pair of rabbit ears set on top for an antenna. We didn't have remote controls so one had to turn the channels by hand. I reached out to the dial and with a flick of the wrist, I turned to Channel Nine to watch my favorite show—the Ray Rayner Show. The show was quite happening for children, mostly because it aired Looney Tunes cartoons. If you don't know Looney Tunes, allow me to "edu-ma-cate ya".

Bugs Bunny, America's favorite smart-assed rabbit was and still is the leader of a cast of zany comic characters. Bugs' trademark: "Eeehh what's up doc? Kept us kids and even adults laughing our heads off. Daffy Duck, Bugs' favorite foil, Porky Pig and Foghorn Leghorn added supporting spice. That Foghorn Leghorn—an over-sized rooster with a certain Kentucky Colonel's accent—used to crack me up. His trademark line of "I say, I say, I say, boy..." was always good for a chuckle or two.

My early morning enthusiasm on this day, however, was largely fueled by the insatiable desire for baseball, particularly baseball highlights. Good ole Ray as we called him, would show all our local teams who played the previous night and since I was eight years old in 1969, I loved to watch my—Chicago Bears, Bulls, Black Hawks, Whites Sox and, of course, the Cubs—the following morning because my bedtime was 8:30 p.m. I needed baseball highlights more than fish need water. You know, from the time I could talk and read, I followed my beloved baseball. The Ray Rayner Show was my kid-tested source for news with a video replay of the late night news, which was later than my eight-thirty bedtime.

My name, by the way, is Christopher Robin Banks and this is a memoir of a simpler time of the life of a happy childhood—well most of the time. I was at the young and impressionable age of eight years old. The year was 1969 in the booming metropolis known fondly as Chi-town to us residents, but Chicago, Illinois to the rest of ya'll. I grew up to be a big sports nut and I'm currently a baseball writer for a major daily paper in Boston. But I would have to point to this year for all it's worth—the thrill ride that the Cubs provided in 1969, which catapulted my love of baseball—a love stronger then my love for my mom's apple pie alamode with Jay's Potato Chips on top.

Noise from the TV in the living room—where I sat in cross-leg position in front of the Zenith—woke up my little brother Jerry. Jerry, who was a light sleeper, was a smaller version of me. He had big blue eyes and sandy hair like me. Jerry entered the living room in his super cool red, white and blue "Amazin' Spiderman" pajamas with the footsies attached. Little brother was seven years old and he joined me on the living room floor of our two-bedroom flat on city's north side.

My mom, Christine (call me Christy) Banks—a petite and beautiful brown-haired woman with a bouffant hairdo and high cheek bones, peeped out of her and my dad's room to see her little angels sitting snugly in front of the TV set. She tugged on her yellow robe close to her bosom and walked out in her yellow fuzzy flip-flops into our kitchen to start making our breakfast.

"You boys want some Frosted Flakes for breakfast?" She asked

40

while reaching into the white metal kitchen cabinets for the cereal.

"Yeah mom," we said in stereo, looking at each other and saying, "They're g-g-r-r-r-r-eaaat!" Just the way Tony "The" Tiger would say it on the now-famous commercials. We laughed but mom shushed us quiet saying we might wake our father still sleeping in the other bedroom.

It was Friday, April 4, 1969—just four days from Opening Day for Major League Baseball—and this would be the year the Chicago Cubs would win the National League pennant, or so we all believed. Actually we believed this at the start of every season. But it was a new season and for all Cub fans of that day hope sprang eternal: "The Cubs will shine in '69."

At least that's what Ernie Banks (no relation), the team's spiritual leader and arguably best player, said at the opening of Spring Training. Banks would say it with a brilliant white endearing smile, a contrast to his dark skin when watching him on our old Black & White telly. Banks was a two-time Most Valuable Player (MVP) for the Cubs in the 1950s and was my hands-down favorite player on the team. The slugging shortstop played on dismal last-place teams and blew out both knees—at age 38, he now plays first base—Banks packed the seats with his stellar play and showmanship.

Jerry and I tuned in to watch Rayner's show religiously—not only for his comic skits and great cartoons—but for sports highlights. Rayner—a rather animated man—talked about the Bulls game and their drive to make the playoffs. We were happy for the Bulls, with Jerry Sloan, Norm Van Lier, Chet Walker and Bob Love, but baseball was our first love. Besides, the Bulls were probably going to lose to the Los Angeles Lakers and Wilt Chamberlain, Jerry West and Elgin Baylor in the playoffs.

Our focus was on America's favorite pastime. Spring had sprung and it was time to let the games begin. Rayner reported the Cubs had packed up their training camp in Scottsdale, Arizona and the team would play a series of exhibition games, which included one in Denver against its minor league club over the weekend. Opening

Day was on Tuesday, April 8. Jerry and I couldn't wait!

School was out for Spring Cleaning but would unfortunately resume on Monday. Now for you old-timers, you might recall, the Cubs played all their home games during the daytime because they didn't have lights. Our chances of seeing the season opener were slim, especially with Fergie Jenkins on the mound. Jenkins, a tall lanky right-handed fire-baller from Canada, was known for pitching 90-minute ballgames. Jerry and I would have to devise a great strategy if we were gonna catch a single pitch of the game.

The grey overcast Saturday had thick cumulus clouds furrowing across the sky. It didn't prevent us kids from playing a pickup baseball game in the school playground. This summer would be the first year of little league ball for many of us on the lot. Of course my best friend Ricky Miller was there. Ricky was a baseball standout. He batted left-handed and threw right-handed, just like his hero, Billy Williams. Billy Williams was a former rookie of the year for the Cubs from Mobile, Alabama, who could launch home run shots over the right field bleachers onto Sheffield Avenue. Ricky could actually hit the ball over the link fence that surrounded our schoolyard. When we chose sides, we always made sure to pick Ricky first.

Me and the guys debated the very idea of the Cubs actually winning the pennant. A Chicago baseball club hadn't accomplished such a feat since 1959—when the Go, Go Sox led by manager Al Lopez did it—but lost the World Series to the Los Angeles Dodgers in six games. Ricky Miller concurred that this was the Cubbies' year.

Rick wagged a long dark finger in the air and said, "Look at their lineup you guys, they have a good leadoff man in Don Kessinger and a great number two hitter in Glenn Beckert. Billy Williams is awesome and (Ron) Santo and Banks at cleanup and fifth are gonna be too cool for school." A streak of white lightning flashed across blackening dark clouds and a big drumbeat of thunder roared after Ricky said it. Dust from the playground swirled in circles and I believed it to be a good omen.

When Ricky Miller spoke, everybody listened. Everyone knew Ricky repeated the snippets of wisdom spoken by his dad and Ricky's dad was a cameraman for WGN sports—the official channel of the Chicago Cubs. Ricky's dad was in Arizona with the Cubs for spring training for a week so he was privy to all the information about who was hot and who was not.

Rain started to fall in light drops as we picked up our ball and bats and gloves and started heading for home. Our parents would be looking for us soon. We all knew it was just a matter of time.

"But what about their pitching? It's kinda thin," Mark Polanski a fourth grader said. "Fergie Jenkins can't do it all alone."

"I think Bill Hands and Ken Holtzman are very good starters and so is Joe Niekro," I chimed in as a clap of thunder roared.

Ricky smiled at me, probably thinking this is one of the reasons that we were best friends. We were the elite baseball minds of the third-grade class and usually agreed on everything.

"The Cubs will do fine in 1969," Jerry cheered and all the guys started rubbing the top of his head and jeered.

"Oh how I wish." Mark said. Indeed Mark.

School on Tuesday was remarkably awful and after we ate lunch it became even more so. The game was scheduled to start at one-fifteen and we didn't get out of school until Three-fifteen. Mr. Branch, the P.E. instructor was listening on his transistor radio during our sixth period gym class from one to two p.m. Mr. Branch, a tall wiry man with huge hands and a booming voice. He encouraged us all compete extra hard for a chance to get close to the radio. Ricky managed to catch the score and told me the Cubs were up 2-0 in the first inning over the Phillies. We had no idea, however, how they got the runs. Excitement permeated the air all day, but the final hour back in the classroom seemed unbearable. I knew there was a good chance we could miss the game completely.

My third grade teacher Mrs. Stampley, treated us to an afternoon of social studies and—don't get me wrong—I think the Serengeti plains are brilliant and beautiful and I always dreamed of visiting lions outside of the zoo, but, I was hoping to see the sweet swing

43

of Billy Williams on a Steve Carlton fastball.

I constantly monitored the clock on the back wall of the classroom, once it reached three o'clock; I nearly sprang out of my chair. I spied across the room where Ricky sat by the window, in a seated sprinter's posture. It was good to see that I wasn't the only one ready to go. Not knowing the score or what inning the game would be in only heightened the suspense. During our lunch break, Ricky, Jerry and I agreed to meet by the north exit near Jerry's room and sprint to our house to see the game. The bell finally sounded and Ricky and I dashed for the coatroom and bypassed our usual ritual of harassment of the girls to meet Jerry.

Ricky and I scooped up Jerry and the race was on to my place. We left our jackets unbuttoned so that they would fly in the breeze like Batman's cape. I would dare say we loved baseball more than Batman, The Green Hornet and Speed Racer combined—at some point we had raced home to watch those programs as well. We darted down Irving Park and up Kenmore Street to Belle Plaine Avenue where our apartment stood on the West side of a yellow brick courtyard building. We could hear an occasional oooh and ahhh from nearby Wrigley Field where the game was being watched live by a capacity crowd of 40,000-plus fans. We piled on top of each other while I rang the doorbell and we waited for my mom to buzz us into the outside security door so we could run upstairs.

"Is that you boys?"

"Yes Mrs. Banks," said Ricky!

We fell over each other giggling and calling each other names as we sprinted up the stairs to the second floor. Mom was waiting with the door open and we all wiped our feet and camped in front of the TV all ready tuned into the game.

"What's the score?" I asked.

"The Cubs are winning 5-3" Mom said idly.

"What inning?" I asked.

She replied. It's the ninth inning, I think.

We were ready to celebrate a rousing Cubs win. When a guy for the Phillies named Don Money stepped to the plate, with a man

44

on base. Money, a Phillies outfielder, drove a Jenkins slider over the right field wall into the bleachers to tie the game.

No!! We all shouted. No way!

Mom came in from the kitchen, we could smell her famous spaghetti sauce full of onions and garlic wafting through the air.

"What happened?"

"They tied the score, mom.

"Oh, dear."

It was past four o' clock and Mom told Ricky to head home before his mom started to worry about him. We said our good-byes and Jerry and I continued to watch the game with sadder faces.

Things got grimmer when Don Money doubled in the leading run in the 11th inning to give Philadelphia a 6-5 lead. It didn't look good for the home team and an opening day crowd of 40,796 began to stream towards the exits for home.

The Cubs didn't go down without a fight, however, in the bottom of the 11th inning Billy Williams led off with a single, while Banks and Santo were both retired. Willie Smith, a pinch-hitter came to the plate as the Cubs' last hope.

Smith yanked a 1-0 pitch into the screaming throngs in the right field bleachers as the Cubs won the game 7-6. Jack Brickhouse, the Cubs' longtime announcer went hoarse screaming "Hey, hey! Hey, hey! The Cubs win! Ooooh brother!'

Jerry and I jumped up and down in the living as mom joined us from the kitchen to celebrate. It was a good day after all. The sun had shone and the Cubs were victorious. Too bad dad wasn't here to see it with us. He was at work, delivering the mail.

Ernie Banks actually had a spectacular opening game for the Cubs. The 38-year-old first baseman hit two, two-run home runs during his first two plate appearances as his dad Eddie Banks came in from Dallas to watch his son play for the first time.

The Cubs were off to a 4-0 start of the season, following a two-game sweep of the Phils and two wins against the Montreal Expos. The Cubs finished the month of April with an impressive 16-7 record and vaulted atop of the National League East standings.

May Flowers

It was Mother's Day in the merry month of May and we were super excited because dad was going to take us to our first baseball game of the season. Yay!!!

Jerry and I couldn't sleep the night before. We laid in our twin side-by-side beds with the covers pulled over our heads—in case dad came in to bust us—whispering about tomorrow.

"Where you wanna sit Jerry?"

"I wanna sit in the dugout." We giggled like little mice in hopes of not being overheard.

"Where do you wanna sit?"

"I wanna sit in the bleachers."

"Why?"

"Ricky's dad took him to the game last year and they sat in the bleachers. He said they had so much fun listening to the fans sing songs, drink beer and heckle the players."

"What does… heck-le mean?"

"It means you shout bad things at a player you don't like—you know—the other team."

"Oh, like, hey Bob Gibson, you stink!"

"Exactly." We hated the St. Louis Cardinals and especially Bob Gibson. They were the World Series runners-up and Gibson single-handedly pitched them to victory. We didn't hate Bob for being good. We just didn't like him beating the Cubs.

"Well you can heckle from anywhere, right?"

"Yeah you can but it's' pose to be more fun out there."

"Why?"

"Cuz Ricky says so."

"Oh." Jerry yawned and covered his mouth with has right hand. "OK".

Before we knew it, we both had drifted off into a deep sleep.

That night, I dreamt about playing in the All-Star game and robbing All-Star slugger Frank Howard of a home run.

I wish you could have seen it. Howard was a 6-foot-8-inch,

three hundred-pound behemoth, who stood in on the right side of the home plate. He was known for hitting home runs clean out of stadiums everywhere. He dug a hole with the spikes of his right shoe and spat tobacco juice in the dirt in the batter's box. He seemed determined to put on a show for his hometown Washington, D.C. fans.

He faced our own Fergie Jenkins on the mound. Fergie, a 6-foot-4 inch, 210-pound right-hander, decided to get ahead in the count and threw a blazing fastball. But big Frank was ready so he hit a drive towards the left field fence—where I was playing—and I raced back to the fence, leapt up like I had rocket boosters in my shoes in time to catch the would-be home run. The crowd was on its feet cheering and Frank, that's what I would call him, just tipped his cap to me. It was really cool. Dreams like that you just don't want to wake up from, you know. A dream come true would be a ticker tape parade for the World Series Champion Chicago Cubs.

Mom was treated to Mother's Day breakfast courtesy of dad. Our father, Jeffrey Banks was a letter carrier for the U.S. Postal Service. He was a baseball player himself, from Valdosta, Georgia. Our mom, Martha Banks, was a Chicago native from the Uptown neighborhood of Chicago. They met one day while dad was jogging on the beach by Lake Michigan.

Our Dad was strong and medium tall man about 5-foot-11, 170 pounds. He had short blond hair styled in a crew cut. He was standing over the stove with mom's apron on, stirring ingredients in the cast iron skillet. He was funny and handsome and everybody liked being around him, including Jerry and me. He was a good teacher as well. He taught me how to ride a bicycle and play sports and how to do math. When we did something well, he would always encourage us in way that made us feel like we could do anything. He had a smile that would light up the room. I wanted to be just like him when I grew up.

My mom was petite athletic woman. She was very kind and loving. She was beautiful with her hair in a bob. She also had a loving smile and the softest touch of anyone I've ever known. She had a way of making everyone she knew feel important, but most importantly, she was generous. She would give our old clothes to neighbors with a new baby or she would bake her to-die-for chocolate chip cookies for the PTA bake sale. She was a pretty great cook, but no one could make Denver omelets like dad. He was treating us all to them today. There was a red rose in a Coke bottle of rectangular wood block kitchen table. And he waved us all to sit at the kitchen table as he prepared the rare delicacies.

Mom was sniffing the flower and smiling at dad like they were in a romantic movie. It was all so weird. I think my dad noticed so he decided to break the spell.

"Hey Jerry, you ready for the game today?"

"Yeah baby"—a strange expression for him, I was bewildered by it. Mom and dad, however nearly fell over with laughter.

The omelets were delicious. Dad split one in half for us kids to share and he and mom ate their own. I was so full from eating just the half an omelet and Jerry couldn't quite finish his half.

"What a great way to start the day." Mom said.

Bright sunshine greeted us as we stepped outside on our walk to Wrigley Field. We were less than four blocks away from the stadium. Mom was dressed in her flower printed yellow mini dress and sandals. Dad wore his blue shorts and blue t-shirt and sandals. Jerry wore his Cubs cap dad bought him last year, blue jeans and white t-shirt and I wore my grey Cubs tee with a big blue team logo in front, blue jeans and sneakers. We headed south on Kenmore to Irving Park where the six-foot high wall of the cemetery lies.

"You know that former heavyweight champion Jack Johnson is buried in here," my father told us pointing to the cemetery's brick wall we were walking beside.

All we could see was a brick wall. But we took his word for it. I never liked walking past here so I just wanted to reach the next corner.

"Who was Jack Johnson, again dad? A boxer?" Jerry asked.

"Yes he was son. He was the first black heavyweight champ from about 1916 to 1922."

"Wow that's older than granddaddy." I said less nervous as got closer to the intersection.

Mom and dad were holding hands as Jerry and I walked ahead and we reached Irving Park and Clark Street, turned left and we could see the flags blowing atop Wrigley Field above the rooftops of the apartment buildings. The wind was blowing out. This bode well for us because it meant we were likely to see some home runs hit today.

The vendors sprang up on the sidewalks, selling Cubs hats, pennants, t-shirts, etc. There were also cotton candy and peanut vendors, but I was still full from the omelet. Jerry's keen eye saw a three-foot high poster of Ernie Banks—a live action snapshot of him holding a bat while standing in the batter's box.

"Dad can we get a poster, please."

"Yeah, please daddy, please."

That baby would look great on the wall between our beds. Dad was in a good mood because he didn't even put up a fight and just went over to stand and bought it for us. Jerry and I did a disjointed happy dance as dad handed me the rolled poster.

As we approached the ticket booth, there wasn't a long line yet because we were still two hours early. We asked to sit in the bleachers but mom said the sun would be too strong for us. We got grandstand seats instead. They were actually great seats—in the first upper deck above the Cubs dugout on the third base side in the first row.

This was some exciting shit for a 8-year-old boy. The rich green grass on the field was perfectly manicured—not like the field in the park. The outfield walls were covered with ivy that was so brilliant green and thick it hung on the wall like an expensive leafy overcoat.

Television, especially black and white television, didn't do this place any justice. TV doesn't reveal all the colors of the fans in the stands and on the field. I wanted to live here.

Wrigley a.k.a. "The Friendly Confines," buzzed with excitement—the chatter from vendors dressed in candy striper-like shirts and hats passed by, hawking food and souvenirs.

"Hey, peanuts. Peanuts here."

"Coke here. Get your coke here."

Many of these vendors were teenagers and how I wished I were older so I could get a job working here. It would be so freaking cool, better than a working vacation.

"You haven't really watched a baseball game live unless you watch batting practice," Dad said to mom, who was sniffing her Mother's Day red corsage.

Jerry and I cheered every Cubs batter during their practice session. The player would stand in the huge fenced-in batting cage at home plate, while one of the coaches, I think it was Joey Amalfatano, threw pitches from behind an L-shaped fence about ten feet in front of the pitching mound.

"Dad, why do players need practice to bat?"

"Well, Jerry because practice makes perfect." Jerry tilted his head as if he didn't quite understand.

"It's like when you do homework," mom jumped in. "Your teacher wants you to practice so when she calls you to the blackboard. If you know the answer, it's like you hit a home run."

"And if you don't, it's like a strikeout," I added.

"Oh, ok. I get it."

Mom just smiled at Jerry and me the whole time we were there. She was so happy. This was a good Mother's Day present for her I could tell.

Ron Santo put on a show during batting practice that day. Santo, the burley third baseman for the Cubs who wore number 10, launched dozens of home run shots, many of which wound up on Waveland Avenue—the street beyond the left field bleachers. He also launched a shot that cleared the green hitting background and into the center field bleachers more than 480 feet away. Wow!

"He has to be very strong to hit like that," I said.

"He must have had his Wheaties!" Jerry added.

For a kid about to complete the first grade, Jerry was cool to hang out with. He would turn seven in October but he was more like my twin brother than my little brother. I couldn't imagine not

50

having him around me. We did everything together.

Batting practice ended and more people filled the aqua blue metal seats. A father and son couple joined our row. They sat by my father who was on the outside, my mom next to him, then Jerry and me. I was on the other aisle.

The father and son were Jim and Tim O'Donnell from Niles. Jim O'Donnell was an older man than my father, with thinning salt and pepper hair hiding underneath a woolen Cubs cap. It was probably from 1945—the last time the Cubs won the pennant. He wore a knit shirt and khaki pants with sporty sandals. Tim was an older boy, almost a man. Turns out he was graduating from Notre Dame High School next week. His son wore Levis blue jeans and white Cubs t-shirt and black canvas Converse All-Stars sneakers.

The O'Donnells and my dad struck up a nice long conversation about baseball right away. It made me a bit jealous, but I played it off.

"Did you hear about Al Lopez's decision to retire," Jim O'Donnell asked my pops, about the Chicago White Sox manager, who skippered the Go-Go Sox of 1959.

"Noooo!" My father replied raising the brim of his cap. "What happened?"

"His health is too bad." Tim answered.

"Yeah I knew he was ailing but I didn't think it was that serious," Dad answered.

"The Sox aren't going to be that good this year so that probably added to his decision," the elder O'Donnell observed.

"Wow-wee," my father said.

The game was a thrilling success for Cub fans an 8-0 victory over the San Diego Padres. Billy Williams hit a two-run blast off Padres hurler Ray Sadecki in the first inning and catcher Randy Hundley followed with a solo shot in the second. The win put rising star pitcher Ken Holtzman's record to 5-1.
The following game was even better, a 19-0 win over the Padres, which tied an NL East record for runs scored. Ernie Banks hit

*two three-run homers and an RBI double for 7 RBI. It was Er-
nie's first home run since Opening Day. Cubs' pitcher Dick Selma
threw a three-hit shutout, which was the Cubs third consecutive
shutout—the first time that happened since 1909. It was also the
most lopsided shutout in NL History, besting the 1906 Cubs vs.
New York Giants and the 1961 Pirates vs. the Cardinals.
The Cubs finished the month of May with a 16-9 record and were
32-16 for the season and, yes, they were comfortably in first place
in the National League East—ahead of those dreaded St. Louis
Cardinals and Pittsburgh Pirates. At this point in the season, the
New York Mets weren't even in the picture.*

June Swoon?

There's a tradition in Chicago baseball lore, which holds particularly true on the North Side: June is the month where a promising
beginning to the season goes up in flames in the summer heat. Ricky
Miller's dad called it the June swoon. He, Ricky's dad, cautioned
us against the impending disappointment to follow the Cubs this
time of year.

"Don't get your hopes up too high Cub fans. They will fade soon.
Mark my words," Mr. Miller said, wagging a cautionary finger in
our direction.

Be that as it may, we couldn't help but get excited about the Cubs
and our own little league baseball season beginning with our first
practice today. Mr. Miller was the manager of our rag-tag group
of wannabe superstars in the making. There was me at second base.
Ricky was the first baseman and pitcher. Jerry was an outfielder—he
grew fond of left field after watching Billy Williams on Mother's
Day. Ricky wanted to play left but his dad convinced him to do
more challenging things.

My dad was an assistant coach because he wasn't sure if his
schedule would permit him to attend all of our games. Dad was a
real baseball star in his youth. Phillip Banks, my dad, played high
school ball in Valdosta, Georgia and was an all-county shortstop

and a pretty good pitcher as well. When we visited my grandparents' house when I was five, my dad's room was like a shrine. He had three-foot high trophies with bronze baseball bats in his room. My grampy told me that dad was a top minor league prospect with the New York Yankees, until he blew out his knee. It's funny that he never brought any of those things to Chicago with him.

My uncle Curtis, who was also a pretty good ballplayer, had moved to Chicago and told my dad to come here and find a job as well. My dad became a mailman—a very good "blue-collar job"—with my uncle. Phillip met Christine one day on the beach one summer. Their eyes met and they both knew they would be together. They tell that story all the time and it makes me wanna vomit. I can't think of my parents as being young and in love. They were my mom and my dad and young lovers, ugh, that word again, made me queasy.

In a couple of more days, the school year would be over and the summer would be upon us. It would be time for picnics, swimming at the beach, and baseball practically every day—major league and little league.

June was not a swoon for the Cubbies. Randy Hundley continued his hot hitting as the first Cub to reach the 10 home run mark for the season. Ken Holtzman was named the player of the month for May, with a 6-1 record and 2.16 ERA in 50 innings of work.

Billy Williams hit a 475 tape measure shot in Atlanta Fulton County stadium and Ernie Banks began a side career as a guest sports columnist with the Chicago Tribune.

Manager Leo Durocher tied the knot on June 19, marrying Lynn Walker Goldblatt. At 63, Durocher, enters in nuptials for the second time in his life.

On June 29, the Cubs celebrated Billy Williams for becoming the National League leader in consecutive games played, topping

St. Louis Cardinals baseball great Stan Musial (896 games). A capacity crowd of 41,060 fans watched the Cubs down the Cardinals 3-1 and 12-8. Between games, Williams received a car, a boat motor, pool table, washer and dryer and made an emotional speech with his wife and family with him.

Ron Santo began his trademark victory celebration by running up the third base line, jumping into the air, and clicking his heels together to celebrate a Cub victory. The Cubs finished the month with a 17-11 record. Whomever said the Cubs would swoon must be on drugs...

Shooting the Moon...

Summertime in the city was in full swing as children everywhere were enjoying their freedom by playing in the park, participating in day camps and traveling with the family for vacation. Our little league team, the Tigers—I know, we wanted the Cubs but they were taken—were undefeated. We were gearing up for a clash with the also unbeaten Expos.

Independence Day was fast approaching so this game was marking the halfway point in our baseball season. I dressed up in my uniform of grey tight-fitting trousers and dark blue shirt and cap. The jersey had the word Tigers across the front and number two on the back. The cap had a T on the front of it. Jerry was putting on his jersey a number three on it, when mom came into the bedroom.

"You boys ready to go?"

"In a minute," I said.

"Okay your father is at the park already so you better get moving.

"Here we come mom.

We bolted out of the room in full uniform and brandished our ball gloves on left hand. I had a bat hoisted over my opposite shoulder. It was a good feeling—the feeling of anticipation before battle, but my stomach was queasy and my heart was pounding so hard I could hear it in my throat when I opened my mouth.

The Tigers played in Belmont Harbor Park. Off in the far off distance you could see the deep blue depths of Lake Michigan. If you were to hit one into the lake, it would be a 3,000-foot homer. Not even Willie McCovey could hit one that far. Thin wispy clouds streaked across a Technicolor blue sky and our love of the game was true. In the distance there were some sailboats and yachts patrolling Lake Michigan.

The field we played on had a big batter's cage around it. There was no home run fence—

another field on the mirrored ours at the other end—

while the infield was mostly dirt. The outfield grass however was nicely manicured.

Our team was stocked with good players but today we had one of our newest guys pitching for us. His name was Manny Blanco. Manny was discovered by sheer luck really. It was during the second game of the season that this longhaired Mexican kid was standing around the foul line on third base, when a foul ball came his way. Manny B—as we now call him—fired a laser like throw to home plate. We all looked at each other in awe as coach (Mr. Miller) ran over to put him on the team right away. The kid had a blazing fastball that no one could touch and my father taught him the curve ball to make him untouchable. Manny flirted with a no-hitter each time he pitched for us.

But it was our hitting that starred in this contest. I had a double, an infield hit and a clean single and scored twice. Jerry had two singles and scored twice and Ricky Miller supplied the power with two homers and a triple as our team, the Tigers tamed the Expos 7-2. Manny pitched five scoreless but the relief gave up two runs. It was party time for us. We had free tacos at Blanco's Mexican restaurant after the game.

The Cubs were still cooking with gas as well. They completed July with a 15-13 record and held a 65-41-1 record overall. Ron Santo was named player of the month for July with a .395 batting average, 6 home runs and 34 runs batted in. Don Kessinger and Santo were voted in as starters in the All-Star Game, while Ernie Banks, Randy Hundley and Glenn Beckert were named to the reserve squad. Banks tied Tris Speaker on the all-time RBI list at 1550.

Oddly enough, Carlos May was the lone selected player for the Chicago White Sox. The National League beat the American League 9-3 at RFK Stadium in Washington, D.C. on July 22nd. All the Chicago players went hitless during the game. Steve Carlton started pitching for the National League and Denny McClain was the starting pitcher for the AL stars. Willie McCovey hit two homers to lead the NL. May of the Sox ended the game with a pinch-hit strikeout against Phil Niekro.

History was made on July 20th, as we watched Walter Cronkite tell us about the moon landing and surface walk by Neil Armstrong. His words— "one small step for man. One giant leap for mankind"—
" will not be forgotten.

August Heat

We arrived on the midnight train to Georgia around eight in the morning and into Atlanta a couple of hours after that. Jerry slept like a baby in the birthing car but I was awake through the wee hours of the morning wondering what adventures we were to encounter. Would we see our friends from down the road, Lefty and Lil Man or would they have moved on. Would our favorite fishing hole be there or would the summer heat have dried up her bountiful waters. And what of Miss Peckinpah, a woman so beautiful that she bewitches young boys—like my kid brother and I—before they are even conscious of her voluptuous pulchritude.

A nice colored man named Cleotus helped us with our mini valise suitcases and led us into the cavernous belly of the station. There were enormous varnished wood benches, taller than both us, and marble floors that were spic and span. An awesome-sized sky window in the ceiling welcomed the Georgia sunshine into the dull décor of brown cedar wood and cement grey walls.

A salt and pepper-haired couple stood in the center of the station waiting calmly until they spotted us. The man was medium height and strong, with a square jaw bushy eyebrows and a broad smile. The woman had her hair pulled back in a bun. She had a kind delicate face like Jerry's. Her appearance was youthful save for the hair and her smile made her appearance almost angelic. She wore a sunflower dress and simple flats and she awaited our charging advances on one knee and wide-open arms. We were so happy to see them both that we nearly knocked grammy over. The first thing she noticed was how much we've grown. My heart jumped for joy and I panted like a playful pup as I hugged my grandpa's leg. They were so happy to see us I could tell and we were overjoyed after a long and uncertain journey to the Deep South.

The drive to Valdosta seemed short and sweet compared to that lengthy train ride but now I began to grow weary. I could finally relax and let my guard down, for I was in the welcoming embrace of my father's mom and dad. I drifted off into a deep sleep to the chatter of Jerry's delighted voice and the warm sun kissing my face against the window of the station wagon.

Upon exploration of our grandparents' farm, we saw a buxom blonde woman strolling down the road. She had a sexy swagger about her that was even irresistible to an eight-year-old. It was none other than Prudence Peckinpaw. My dad says she was Jane Mansfield's stand-in in a movie once. I didn't really know who Jane Mansfield was but she must've been something really special. She was medium height with a breast package that would have been magnificent in my breast-feeding years. Jerry and I immediately stopped in our tracks, swooning in her radiance as she beckoned to us. Jerry busted out into a dead sprint and smashed into Miss Peckinpaw's huge cushiony bosoms. I couldn't let Jerry have all the fun so I made my bid in a place of warmth. Jerry and I nearly knocked her over from the impact.

"G'mornin' boys. Isn't a glorious day? Her Dixie accent still deep and throaty and her voice as effervescent as I remembered. I grinned from ear to ear at her—a dumb and silly grin. Frankly it was a new face I've discovered, it was probably a face of arousal, if a kid my age could get aroused.

She stepped back to look at us. Ya'll look just fine. Handsome like yo' daddy. How's he doin' by the way?

He's fine. We chimed in together. I still had traces of a grin on my face.

"Well ya'll enjoy your stay here and stop by the house to see me this weekend. I'm baking apple pies.

We looked at each other hungry and horny. Ah Ok ma'am."I finally found my voice.

She giggled to herself a bit. Probably amused she can cast a spell on those so young and innocent. She walked away giving us the rearview—also quite plump and we just moaned and fell backwards onto the lawn.

Miss Peckinpaw and Jerry always seemed to have a more special bond and it became more special for Jerry because she was the woman who taught Jerry the ways of love on his sixteenth birthday.

Life with our grandparents was really good. I forgot about baseball almost completely. We learned to milk a cow and gather eggs from a hen house and after chores we went swimming in the creek just a half a mile behind their house. We were unable to watch the Cubs broadcasts for the month because our grandparents didn't own a television. We listened to the radio in the evening and grampy would tell stories about fighting in World War II with General Patton. Our grampy was a kind man who never raised his voice. He never laid a hand on my father or uncle Curtis. He said he had done enough harm in the war. So he'd just sit them down and talk to them and they did what ever he'd say.

My grammy was a small woman with strong hands. She would raise her voice but usually to call us in the house for supper. She made the best buttermilk biscuits and gravy and chicken fried steak.

The time with our grandparents flew by and we were sorry to

leave the wide-open spaces of Georgia. As grampy would say: "All good things must come to an end and they did.

The Cubs were a very good 18-11 for the month of August but showed some signs of not slowing down. Some highlights:

On August 17th the Cubbies helped Fergie Jenkins to his 17th win of the season against the San Francisco Giants during a thrilling eighth inning rally. Paul Popovich hit a clutch pinch-hit single to clear the way. Fergie tossed a three-hit gem.

On the 19th, the Cubs beat the Chicago White Sox 2-0 during the annual exhibition to benefit boys baseball. Ernie Banks and Billy Willliams each homered in a jam-packed Comiskey Park on Chicago's south side.

Cubs' pitcher Kenny Holtzman threw a no-hit, no run game on August 20th in a 3-0 victory over, whom else, the Atlanta Braves, but this game was played before 41,033 Wrigley Field faithful. Our grandfather's main man, Hank Aaron, gave fans a scare in the seventh inning when he launched a blast toward the left field stands against the wind that Billy Williams caught against the vines. Ron Santo did manage to reach the left field catwalk with a blast—Santo's 25th homer of the season came off Hall of Fame knuckle baller Phil Neikro.

However, Cubs fans they closed the month losing four in a row. They split a double-header in Houston and then dropped three straight games to Cincinnati. They closed the month losing to none other than Hank Aaron and the Atlanta Braves 5-4 in a game where Hammerin' Hank hit his 37th homer of the season and 547th of his distinguished career.
The division leading Cubs' lead was reduced to a mere 3 ½ games.

A SEPTMEBER TO REMEMBER

It can now be called a September to remember, however for Cubs fans for the next four decades it became a September that they'd just as soon forget.

When we were with the grandparents in Atlanta, Jerry, Grandpa and I listened to three Cubs—Braves contests. We clinched our but cheeks and felt time freeze when Hank Aaron hit the shot off Holtzman during the no-hit game and we did the twist when Billy Williams caught it. I had started to feel my confidence in the Cubs' invulnerability start to wane and I kept it to myself but I had a deep sinking feeling in the pit of stomach.

They began September with a road trip in Cincinnati against Sparky Anderson's Reds where they won a double-header 5-4 and 8-2 and they expanded their lead to 6 games in the division over the New York Mets. Jenkins won a league-tying 19th game in second game.

Meanwhile the Mets were beginning a West Coast road show that would amaze fans in years to come. They would sweep the Los Angeles Dodgers. Back in Cincinnati, a guy named Jim Mahoney pitches the game of his life—a two-hit shutout in a 2-0 victory. This loss became bad news for the Cubs because the wound up losing four in a row. They dropped three to Pittsburgh at Forbes Field and the Mets had reduced the lead in the division down to 3 ½ games again.

This set the stage for a crucial three-game series in New York's Shea Stadium between the two. Prior to this season, the Mets were a franchise expansion club that had broken into the league at the beginning of the decade. They had never finished better than last place. They enlisted the service of Brooklyn Dodgers hero Gil Hodges to manage the Club and they grew some talent in the minor league system that began to blossom. Pitchers like Tom Seaver, Jerry Koosman, Nolan Ryan, Tug McGraw would become memorable players in their future. Position players such as Cleon Jones, Tommy Agee and Ron Swaboda would impress with their defensive prowess and timely hitting.

It was September 10th and Jerry and I would stay up to watch each and every game with our dad. I was never a superstitious person until I watched the first game of the series. In the very first inning of the game, the Cubs were batting, when suddenly a black cat walked onto the field and headed towards the Cubs' dugout. Grown men scattered for cover trying not to let bad luck kitty rub off on them. The Cat seemed to be getting a kick out of it because he sauntered the length of the dugout defying these mere mortals daring them to pet him. And as suddenly and astonishingly as he appeared, he took off toward the outfield and through a gate in right field. New York fans let out a roar that was sarcastic and inspired and that pretty much tells the story for the Cubs in that series. The Mets swept the Cubs in all three games and the lead was reduced to a ½ game. They dropped three more in Philadelphia to fall out first place for the first time since May and they went on to lose a painstaking eleven out of twelve more contests. We couldn't watch it anymore but we could here a new cuss word coming from the living room and our dad. It was pretty awful to tell the truth.

The Mets went on to win the National League East pennant and yes, the World Series. I think they were called the Amazing Mets or the Miracle Mets, I forget the details. The Cubs, ironically never quite recovered from that season, went on to become the loveable losers. I can remember in 1971, begging and pleading with my father to move our family to Los Angeles or New York so we could win some championships for once. He respectfully declined, telling us that we could not abandon our home because we hit a rough patch in life. It was more like a rough acre in life.

Author's note:

I miss those days in 1969, we were young and innocent then, quite simply. And more than any other time in American sport, we were colorblind.

The class of '69 transcended the racial divide. The only color that mattered was the lush green ivy on the Wrigley field walls. Cubs announcers Jack Brickhouse, Lou Boudreau and sportscaster Wendell Smith were a symbol behind the scenes of the potential of that year. Brickhouse was a man who made the Cubs games exciting and wonderful even during the darkest summer nights. He preached loyalty and understanding and of better tomorrows. I salute you Jack, Hey Hey...

I will always love honor and cherish that team and never forget the gifts you gave us. It wasn't the championship but I understand that everything happens for a reason. And when the Cubbies finally win the World Series, the city of Chicago will have a party so big, the city will be hung-over for years to come.